For
Michael John

J.C.

For
Mum and Dad

S.L.

First published 1993 by
Walker Books Ltd
87 Vauxhall Walk
London SE11 5HJ

Text © 1993 June Crebbin
Illustrations © 1993 Stephen Lambert

Printed and bound in Hong Kong by
South China Printing Co. (1988) Ltd

This book has been typeset
in Goudy.

British Library Cataloguing in
Publication Data
A catalogue record for this book
is available from the British Library.

ISBN 0-7445-2245-5

FLY BY NIGHT

Written by June Crebbin

Illustrated by Stephen Lambert

WALKER BOOKS
LONDON

Once, at the edge of a wood, lived two owls, a mother owl and her young one, Blink. Every day, all day long, they slept. Every night, all night long, the mother owl flew and Blink waited.

One day,
when the sun
was still low in the sky, Blink opened
one eye and said, "Now? Is it time?"
"Soon," said his mother. "Soon.
Go back to sleep."

Blink tried
to sleep.

When the sun rose and warmed the earth,
he opened the other eye. "*Now* is it time?"
"Not yet," said his mother. "Soon.
Go back to sleep."

Blink tried.

Butterflies looped and drifted
past him. Beetles scuttled in the
undergrowth. Near by, a
woodpecker tapped on
a tree trunk.

Blink couldn't sit still.

"Is it time *yet?*" he said.

His mother opened her eyes.

"You are old enough and strong

enough –" Blink dithered with

excitement – "but you must wait."

His mother closed her eyes.

The sun was at its highest.
A squirrel leapt from tree to
tree, quicker than a thought.
Along Blink's branch it came,
right past him, its tail
streaming out behind.
Blink wriggled and jiggled.
He *couldn't* sit still.

All that long afternoon, he watched and waited. He shuffled and fidgeted. Below, in the clearing, a deer and its fawn browsed on leaves and twigs. High above, a kestrel hovered, dipped and soared again into the sky. "When will it be *my* time?" said Blink to himself.

Towards dusk, a sudden gust
of wind, sweeping through
the wood, lifting leaves on
their branches, seemed to
gather Blink from his branch
as if it would lift him too.
"Time to fly," it seemed to say.
Blink fluffed out his feathers.
He shifted his wings.

But the wind swirled by.

It was all puff and nonsense.

Blink sighed. He closed his eyes.

The sun slipped behind the fields.

The moon rose pale and clear.

A night breeze stirred. "Time to fly."

"Puff and nonsense," muttered Blink.

"*Time to fly*," said his mother beside him.

Blink sat up. "Is it?"

he said. "Is it? *Really?*"

The grey dusk had deepened.

Blink heard soft whisperings.

He saw the stars in the sky.

He felt the dampness of the

night air. He knew it was

time to fly. He gathered his

strength. He drew himself up.

He stretched out his wings and –

lifted into the air.

Higher and higher.

He flew. Further and further.

Over the wood, over the fields,

over the road and the sleeping city.

High in the sky, his wing-beats strong,

Blink flew on over the sleeping city –

and over the fields and the winding river.

His first flight; a fly-by-night.